Paul Hunt's
NIGHT
Diary

Child's Play (International) Ltd
Swindon   Bologna   New York
© 1992 M. Twinn   ISBN 0–85953–925–3   Printed in Singapore
Library of Congress Number 92-10850

High summer sunset.
The last light burns in the bedroom.

10.15 p.m.

A water shrew sniffs at a snail.

A badger lumbers through the woods.

10.30 p.m.

A grass snake rustles through the undergrowth.
Its forked tongue tastes the air.

On the opposite bank, a nesting swan.

10.45 p.m.   Mute swans:
a pen on her nest of sticks;
a cob diving for food.

The pen hisses.
Has someone come too near?

11.00 p.m.

A sickly scent, out of place
among the leafy smells of the forest,
leads us to the river.

Perfume . . .
People enjoying the magic of night.

A male great crested newt
swims past their feet.

11.45 p.m.

A fox in the long grass.

A stray cockerel suspects nothing.

Two lambs suckling.

12.00 Midnight.

All is quiet.

An osprey drops like a stone
to snatch a salmon
from the base of the waterfall.

With a satisfied whistle,
it soars again
and climbs to its eyrie.

12.15 a.m.

Four goats.
A kid suckling.

Calm before the storm.

12.30 a.m. Rabbits.
A buck and a doe foraging.

The buck's ears prick in alarm
at the drone of a distant car engine.

Too late . . .
He freezes in the headlights' glare.

The doe twitches nervously.
Storm clouds gather.
A distant rumbling of thunder.

12.45 a.m.

A mole emerges from his hole
and catches the first droplet of rain.

The doe darts into her warren.
Where is her mate?

A green woodpecker
pops out his head from the nest,
and mutters at the rain.

A clump of mushrooms.
Their smell is overpowering.
Like radishes.

1.00 a.m.

A bolt of lightning strikes
a decaying beech tree.
Forks of lightning
play among the leafless branches.

1.15 a.m.

Horses and donkeys.

A horse drinks at the water's edge.
In the distance, the clouds are gathering pace.

1.45 a.m.

Reeds bend almost to breaking point
in the fierce wind.

A windmill turns vigorously.

2.00 a.m.

Friesian cows bow, concerned,
over a dead fawn, a victim of the storm.

2.45 a.m.

A barn owl leaves its perch
in the trees.
Something moved in the grass
on the river bank.

The owl turns,
crescent-shaped, in the moonligh

A harvest mouse nibbles, unaware,
as the owl swoops over the footbridge.

2.46 a.m.

The owl soars over the river bank
with its prey.

3.00 a.m.

Another catch.
A kingfisher with a stickleback.

Bats leave their roost in ruined castle walls
to feast on insects on the water's surface.

3.15 a.m.

Who else could be about at this time?

A poacher emerges from the bushes,
rifle in one hand, flashlight in the other.
The beam hurts our eyes.
The poacher hasn't seen the deer yet.

3.45 a.m.

Dawn patrol.

Dragonflies skim the water,
only hours after emerging from their nymphal cases.

Below the surface,
fish wait their chance to catch an insect.

4.00 a.m.

A scavenging raven picks at
the remains of a buck rabbit . . .

Another casualty of the night.

Morning dew on a spider's web.

4.30 a.m.

The sun begins to rise.

A mallard and her young
caught in its rays.

5.00 a.m.

Dawn chorus.
The thrush greets a new day.